Hansello
&
Gertrude

A Hood Fable

Hansello & Gertrude

WRITTEN BY: LADELL BEAMON
ILLUSTRATED BY: AARON LIDDELL

ARPress
ILLUMINATING IDEAS.
EMPOWERING VOICES

ARPress
45 Dan Road Suite 36
Canton MA 02021

Hotline: 1(888) 821-0229
Fax: 1(508) 545-7580

Ordering Information:
Quantity Sales. Special discounts are available on quantity purchases by corporations, associations, and others. For details, contact the publisher at the address above.

Printed in the United States of America.

ISBN-13   Softcover   979-8-89356-795-3
                    eBook   978-1-64961-964-8

Library of Congress Control Number: 2021922322

Once upon a time in a hood not too far from you in the heart of South Memphis lived the 14th and 15th children of Larry and Shauntae Edwards, Hansello and Gertrude. Like any other children, Hansello and Gertrude loved eating candy. Now you know like I know in the stereotypical urban "hood" there's a candy lady. The children from the community loved eating candy apples, pickles, moon pies, hot fries, strawberry cookies and freeze cups from the neighborhood candy lady, Ms. Mable.

Ms. Mable had to leave the community because her mother in Mississippi got extremely ill. This left all neighborhood boys and girls very disappointed, until the day that Madam Gazelle moved in six (6) miles outside of South Memphis. It was rumored that Gazelle was a witch who ate her grandchildren for dinner when their mother went creeping with one of her seven (7) baby's daddys. Hansello and Gertrude's parents warned them to never go to Madam Gazelle's for anything. However like any other child, the more you tell them not to do something the more tempted they are to do it.

Four days had passed since, they received their warning, but Hansello and Gertrude the youngest of Larry and Shauntae's children decided to get their hopes set on going to visit Madam Gazelle's candy shop. Now rumor has it that since Madam Gazelle's candy shop opened, seven (7) children from South Memphis had been reported missing. Hansello and Gertrude heard the rumors from Pops at Mom and Pops' corner store.

Mrs. Edwards asked her youngest children Hansello & Gertrude to pick up some cold cuts from Mom and Pops corner store for lunch on this particular Saturday morning.

They both got excited and took this as a chance to sneak off to Madam Gazelle's candy shop. Unfortunately, they never thought about the distance or the warnings that they had been given. Not thinking as most children do when they get excited, Hansello and Gertrude went straight to Mom and Pops' corner store to order the cold cuts.

Running into Leroy who was on his way back to the neighborhood from his purchase of magical turnip green seeds, he advised them to visit this mysterious hustler. He told them of his purchase of magical seeds and they were amazed at what they heard!

Upon arriving at Mom and Pops' corner store, Hansello and Gertrude quickly came upon the mysterious hustler who knew about their plans to visit Madam Gazelle's candy shop. At this point, the children were amazed at the hustler's knowledge of their plans seeing that they had told no one.

The hustler quickly told them that they would need to take some glow in
the dark jaw breakers to drop along the way to Madam Gazelle's in case
it got too dark and they got lost.
Hansello insisted that they would be back before dark because they had
to get back home for lunch.

The hustler shook his head and told them that he would rent them a magical iPod to jam to so they could move faster and he would also throw in the magical jawbreakers for free!

Gertrude wanted to know what he wanted in exchange for the items.His request was a little bit on the strange side.The hustler told them this story about some magical break dancing gingerbread men who gave free lessons right before you eat them.

He said he needed them because the Hood Fables Book would paint him as a weird guy and he wanted his next gig to be with America's Next Best Dance Crew. He also told them to bring him back four (4) of them so they could perform Dancing Machine by the Jackson 5.

Hansello and Gertrude quickly took the deal and went inside of Mom and Pops to place their order for two dollars' worth of rag bologna, two dollars' worth of ham, two dollars' worth of hot souse and four dollars' worth of hook cheese.That left them with 5 dollars to visit Madam Gazelle's.

Gertrude put on the headphones to the iPod and started jamming Beyoncé's "Party". She quickly followed behind Hansello as he took short cuts in the direction of Madam Gazelle's. Everything was going fine until it started to get dark all of a sudden. Gertrude took off her headphones and asked Hansello about the time. She had only listened to Beyoncé's "Party" and Black Eye Pea's "Get the Party Started". It could not have gotten dark that quick.

Hansello looked at his watch and told her that three (3) hours had passed. He too knew something was strange and asked Gertrude if she would like to turn around.Gertrude told him that they were in trouble regardless so they might as well finish what they started.

She asked him if he still had the glow in the dark jaw breakers. He said, "Yes", and pulled the jawbreakers from a bag in his pocket.Hansello and Gertrude continued on their journey to Madam Gazelle's while dropping the magical jaw breakers along the way.

They knew when they had arrived at Madam Gazelle's because they could smell the baked cookies coming from the house that was shaped like a strawberry cupcake. They both went to the door and were greeted by a young lady who looked like a dancer from In Living Color's Fly Girls.

The children quickly entered the door while the door rapidly closed by itself behind them. Because they were enchanted by the smell they never noticed the door closing behind them, the magical chimes ringing in their ears, or the fat kids in cages with chocolate dripping from their lips.

The last thing they remembered was entering into the cupcake designed house and seeing a young lady that looked like a fly girl dancer from "In Living Color" that has now changed into a six foot 9 inch hideous witch with a huge wart on her nose. She led them to the cookie house where they ate strawberry cookies, lemon cookies, pineapple cookies and butter cookies.

Madam Gazelle looked upon them with greed in her eyes as Hansello and Gertrude the 14th and 15th children of Larry and Shauntae Edwards began to get fatter and fatter within minutes. Madam Gazelle turned up her hidden furnace so she could immediately cook the children, but suddenly out popped these four break dancing gingerbread men.

One of the gingerbread men noticed an iPod on Gertrude's waist and quickly hit the play button while Madam Gazelle was distracted. Michael Jackson's "Wanna Be Starting Something" quickly came on causing Hansello and Gertrude to snap out of the trance and realized what was happening. The gingerbread men started dancing which magically triggered every captured child and person including Madam Gazelle "The Witch" to start dancing uncontrollably.

The children started losing weight and sweating off pounds. The witch was dancing as she attempted to try to capture the children that were now skinny enough to slip through the cage bars.

The gingerbread men led Hansello, Gertrude and the rest of the children out of the baking room. Hot on their tails, the witch slipped on the sweat of the dancing children and fell into the oven.

The gingerbread men led the children to freedom as the cupcake house vanished into thin air. Hansello and Gertrude generously thanked the Gingerbread men and told them about the mysterious hustler who wanted them to teach him how to break dance. They agreed to go with them as Hansello begin looking for the glow in the dark jawbreakers.

He could not find a single one. Right when he was about to panic, a huge wolf jumped out and begin to talk to them. He told them that he had met a young lady that was on her way to her grandmother's house to kick it with her, when he started eating these glowing jaw breakers. He said that he was just about to eat her until all but four (4) of his sharpest teeth fell out.

He asked if they knew who dropped the jawbreakers. Hansello replied, "me"! The wolf said, "that's all I needed to know". The Wolf put in his false teeth and began to chase them all.

In the middle of the chase, Gertrude's iPod alarm goes off and she finds herself and Hansello back at Mom and Pop's corner store picking up the cuts. It was now 12:30 in the after- noon and everything was back to normal. Hansello and Gertrude walked out of the store, looked at each other and said," forget them cookies let's go home".

Moral of the Story:
A moment spent making the right decisions can save you from a lifetime of danger.